D0130802

# PORKELIA

## A Pig's Tail

A Mackinac Island Book
Published by Charlesbridge
85 Main Street
Watertown, MA 02472
(617) 926-0329
www.charlesbridge.com

Rockette and the Rockettes are trademarks of Radio City Trademarks LLC.

Library of Congress Cataloging-in-Publication Data on file

Fiction

ISBN 978-1-934133-28-6

Summary: Porkelia the pig pursues her dream to become a Piggy Rockette, no matter the obstacles in her way.

Designed by Elizabeth Eddins, eddinsdesign, Providence, RI

Printed September 2010 by Imago in Singapore

10 9 8 7 6 5 4 3 2 1

This book is dedicated to my sons,
Max and Luke.

Porkelia could kick her hoof
high in the air,
but her spirit was heavy
with angst and despair.
Once it was true
that mud-rooting thrilled,
but Porkelia was now
a pig unfulfilled!

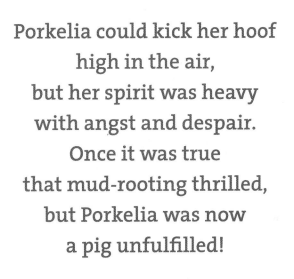

She turned to the Wise One
in search of an answer;
the Wise One declared,
"You're a born piggy dancer!
Not just any old hoofer,
my sweet pink coquette,
you're destined to be
the first piggy Rockette!"

Relieved of her sadness,
her anguish and doubt,
she kicked her hoof high,
and twirled on her snout!
Porkelia told friends
she would soon be a star,
and would ride in the back
of a limousine car!

"The crystal ball showed
my name up in lights.
I'll dazzle the world
in sequins and tights!"
The other pigs squealed,
"That Wise One's a sham!
You'll end up as dinner –
an apple-stuffed ham!"

But Porkelia stood firm;
she remained resolute,
and purchased, on sale,
a gold dancing suit.
She added some tap shoes
in ooh-la-la red,
and fashioned a star hat
to sit on her head.

The hat was faux gold
and spelled out her name,
with a star that blinked twice
when she pulled on a chain.
Slowly, the others
accepted her dream.
They stopped being
boorish, snotty and mean!

A sty bash was held,
all gathered about,
to applaud as Porkelia
kicked hoof and twirled snout.
The next day at dawn
she left all alone.
She tearfully promised
that she would phone home.

She walked for one mile,
then for two miles more,
but her ooh-la-la shoes
left her tired and sore.
She soon would have traded
the star on her head
for a sty of warm mud,
and some hay for a bed.

Turning off her star hat,
she slumped down and cried,
"I won't be a Rockette,
if I can't find a ride!
How will I become
a big dancing star,
if I can't catch a train,
a bus or a car?"

But when destiny calls,
there is always a way,
and a taxi appeared
the very next day!
The lights of the city
soon lifted her gloom,
and she rented a
soon-to-be Rockette-type room.

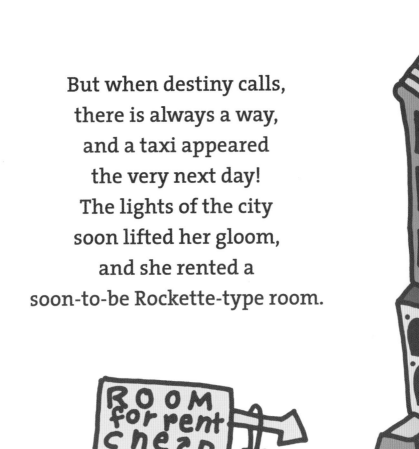

As the sign out the window
flashed Earl's Bar & Grill,
Porkelia grew homesick
for cornhusks and swill.
With fame still a dream
for this former sty pig,
she sold blenders by day
and by night danced her gig.

Porkelia worked hard
as a means to an end,
selling kitchen machines
that puree, chop and blend.
But she often had doubts,
misgivings and fears,
of a life selling blenders
as months turned to years.

She started to doubt
what the Wise One had said,
and spent long lonely days
sobbing in bed.
Then one afternoon
at the Blender World Store,
a Rockette-type agent
appeared at the door!

"I watched you kick hoof
at last night's late gig,
I'm sure I can make you
a star dancing pig!"
She became a Rockette
as the Wise One foretold,
and soon danced on stage
in costumes most bold.

Standing proud in the line,
she kicked hoof with the girls,
then the star pig alone
aced her snout twirls.
Though the other girls tried
to twirl on their noses,
they ended up twisted
in unsightly poses!

As Porkelia performed
all over the world,
the tabloids declared
her tail "Surgically Curled!"
Despite all the gossip,
she kept her good cheer,
and paid cash for a home
with a pink chandelier.

She had tea with the Queen,
and ate lunch with a czar,
and she rode in the back
of a limousine car.
She appeared in a show
on Shopping TV,
selling exercise bikes
and rings filigree.

Porkelia loved stardom,
of this there's no doubt,
but she never forgot
she had hooves and a snout.
One day in late June,
on her gold lamé phone,
the star kept her promise
and called her old home.

"I want you to know –
I'm not destitute,
I've become a Rockette
in a sparkly tight suit!
Please come and see me
kick high on the stage,
the Wise One was right,
I am now all the rage!"

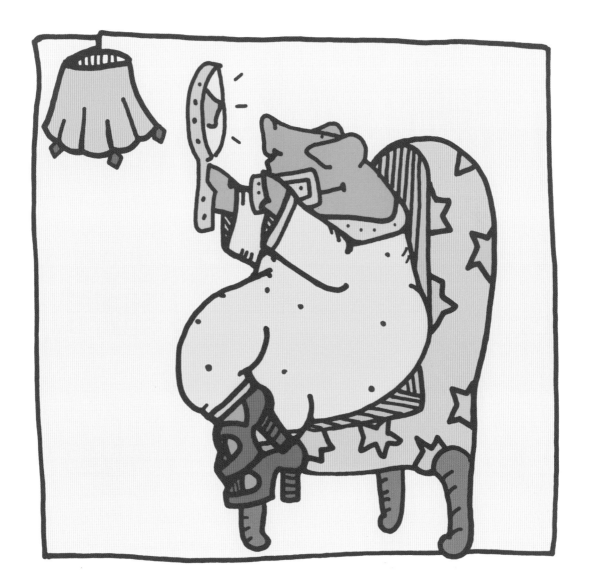

"I'm sending my bus,
The Porkelia Express,
to bring my sty friends
to my Rockette address."
After buying new clothes
at The Fabulous Swine,
her friends climbed on board,
looking stylish and fine.

They arrived at the theatre
in time for the show,
and were ushered to seats
in the very first row.
When Porkelia appeared,
dressed in true Rockette style,
the pigs squealed with delight –
and rolled in the aisle!

The pigs in Row One
continued to shout,
as Porkelia flipped twice
from her hoof to her snout.
When the star pig performed
eighteen hoof-snout rotations,
the pigs leaped from their seats
for a standing ovation!

They chatted backstage
about days in the sty,
until it was time
for a tearful goodbye.
Waving their hooves
as the bus headed home,
the pigs promised their star
they'd remember to phone.

When the pigs returned home,
their hearts filled with joy,
they created and sold
a Porkelia Pig Toy!
The money from sales
helped A Styful of Dreams,
which championed piglets
of limited means.

Years down the road,
when Porkelia retired,
she remained a role model,
a pig who inspired!
She opened ten dance schools
in Jersey and France,
teaching talented piglets
to snout-twirl and dance.

She watched as they danced
in ooh-la-la red,
with small golden star hats
on each little head.

And *one* of those piglets,
if most resolute,
may became a Rockette
in a sparkly tight suit!

The End

Although this is a small book, it required a
big effort and the help of others to complete.

Special thanks to:
Elizabeth Eddins, of eddinsdesign;
Cathie DeCesare, my business manager;
Anne Lewis, Publisher, Mackinac Island Press;
Arthur Votolato; Leah Waterman; Liz Sanger;
Jan Garbutt; Liisa Silander; and the
friends and family who supported my efforts.

And also:
Mr. William Kushner, a teacher who long ago said
the right words at the right time.